Marky Polo's Travels
Marky Polo
in
Singapore

WRITTEN BY **EMILY LIM-LEH** • ILLUSTRATED BY **NICHOLAS LIEM**

NEW JERSEY • LONDON • SINGAPORE • BEIJING • SHANGHAI • HONG KONG • TAIPEI • CHENNAI • TOKYO

A Guide to Experiencing Augmented Reality in This Book

1  Download WSE+ app.

2  Activate by scanning this book's barcode. Then, tap on the book cover image on your screen.

3  Scan and hold camera over scanned page to see AR. Wherever you see this icon, scan the whole page.

SnapLearn is compatible with devices running minimally on iOS 8 and Android 5.0 with gyroscope. For the best AR experience, please scan the physical or PDF version of the book. For any app-related issues, please contact us via email at hello@snaplearn.com.

Powered By :

Dear Travel Diary,
I come from a line of famous travellers.
Our family adopts first names based on what each of us is good at:

My great grandparents are fearless adventurer Macho Polo and top martial arts fighter Muay Thai Polo.

My grandparents are Matcha and Miso Polo, top experts on Japanese tea and seasoning.

My parents are Masala and Mala Polo, largest collectors of spices in the world.

My younger cousin Merry Polo is coming to Singapore. How do I keep her occupied? Help!

Marky Polo
(Trying to make my mark in the world...
Mark my words, I will discover what I am good at!)

Great-grandfather **Macho Polo** — the first and only pangolin to scale to the top of Mount Everest. He met his match in great-grandmother **Muay Thai Polo**, top martial arts fighter from Thailand.

Grandfather **Matcha Polo** and grandmother **Miso Polo** discovered their love for Japan when they travelled there. Matcha Polo became an expert in green tea and Miso Polo an expert in Japanese food seasoning.

Father **Masala Polo** travelled to India and built up the largest spice collection in the world there. Mother **Mala Polo** shares his love of spices, but of the spicy, Sichuan tongue-numbing kind, from her China travels.

Merry Polo is the most merry-making (and sometimes least thoughtful) traveller in the family!

Marky Polo is playing tourist guide in Singapore for the first time.

Merli and his friends are ambassadors of Singapore. They love welcoming visitors!

"Merli, thanks for offering to show my cousin, Merry, around Singapore," Marky said. "I have no idea where to begin."

Merli grinned. "There's no need to thank me, Marky. That's what friends are for!"

"Oh, Merry's flight has landed," Marky said. "Let's get her."

As they turned to go, someone jumped out from behind them.

4

Jewel Changi Airport is home to more than 2,000 trees and over 100,000 shrubs from around the world. Right in the heart of Jewel stands the HSBC Rain Vortex. At 40-metres high, it is the world's tallest indoor waterfall.

6

Merry shoved her luggage to Marky as she questioned Merli.

7

"Let's go down those slides!" Merry cried.

"I'm not the sliding sort," Marky protested as Merry dragged him along.

"Let's try the Walking Net too!" Merry exclaimed.

"Look! Some parts of the Walking Net hang over five floors of air and you can see all the way down to Level 1!" Merli said.

Merry bounced her way to the other side and hopped off.

"Come on! Let's check out the Mirror Maze!" Merry cried.

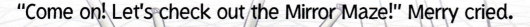

Canopy Park features the first-of-its-kind indoor wonderland, with fun play attractions such as bouncy nets, exciting mazes and giant slides. Complete your experience with a stroll at the Petal Garden and Topiary Walk.

"I can't wait to explore all of Singapore! Where are we headed next?"

"We're heading to Gardens by the Bay. My friend, Chomp Chomp will meet us there," Merli said.

Chomp Chomp? He sounds like a big eater!

Yes, he loves food!

 "Hi, Chomp Chomp! You brought my favourite kaya toast!" Merli exclaimed. "Thanks!"

"You're welcome!" Chomp Chomp replied. Turning to Merry, he asked, "Ready for a good walk?"

Merry tagged Chomp Chomp and sped off.

"We'll meet you at Cloud Forest!" Chomp Chomp hollered to Marky and Merli as he lumbered after Merry.

11

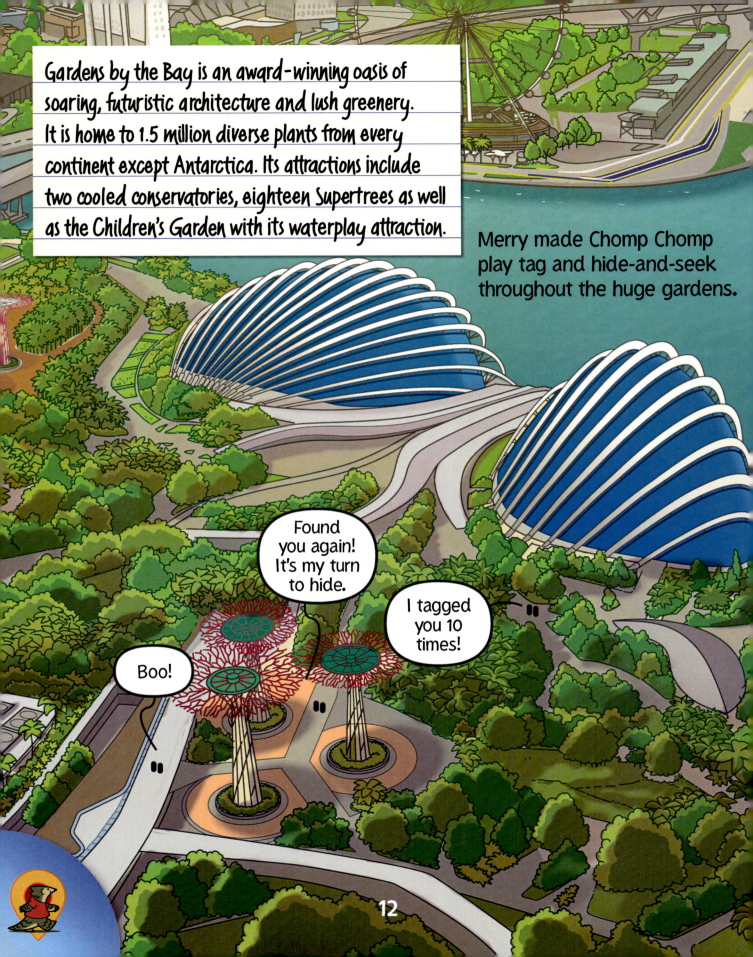

Gardens by the Bay is an award-winning oasis of soaring, futuristic architecture and lush greenery. It is home to 1.5 million diverse plants from every continent except Antarctica. Its attractions include two cooled conservatories, eighteen Supertrees as well as the Children's Garden with its waterplay attraction.

Merry made Chomp Chomp play tag and hide-and-seek throughout the huge gardens.

Found you again! It's my turn to hide.

I tagged you 10 times!

Boo!

By the time Merli and Marky caught up with them, Chomp Chomp was winded.

Merry, however, had caught her second wind inside the gigantic cooled conservatory.

"Let's see who reaches the top of Cloud Forest first!" She skipped off, without waiting for anyone.

Marky, Merli and Chomp Chomp scurried to keep up.

"Awesome view!" Marky said as he reached the top.

"Dinner would be awesome too," Chomp Chomp said when his tummy rumbled.

Oh... chow time! What are we waiting for?

Wait! I want to enjoy the view.

"You can run and enjoy the view at the same time," Merry said, pulling Marky along.

13

When they reached Satay by the Bay food centre, Chomp Chomp's stomach was growling.

"I'll take all the satay you have, please," Chomp Chomp told the satay seller.

Really?

Hmm... I'm not sure if we'll make it back to the Supertrees in time for the light and sound show.

"Aww... we have to!" Merry cried as she gulped down her dinner. Then, she leapt up. "Chomp up and let's go!"

"Wait!" Chomp Chomp said, grabbing a handful of satay and hurrying along.

Garden Rhapsody is the signature light and sound show at Gardens by the Bay. These free daily night shows incorporate the spectacular Supertrees and are regularly refreshed with different themed song medleys.

So, what merriment is on for tomorrow?

"This is magical!" Merry exclaimed.

15

The next day, Merli and Marky took Merry to Kampong Gelam.

"Jewel is our expert on arts and culture," Merli told Merry.

"She's our 'culture vulture'," Marky added.

"I am a hornbill, really," Jewel said with a laugh.

Kampong Gelam, Singapore's historic Muslim quarter, has evolved into a centre for arts and culture. At the same time, the neighbourhood remains deeply rooted in history, offering visitors a taste of Singapore's past and present.

Merry stared closely.

Quiz time! See those black bands below Sultan Mosque's golden domes? What material are they made of?

Are those glass bottle ends?

The base of Sultan Mosque's golden domes are decorated with glass bottle ends, donated by lower-income Muslims during its construction, so that all Muslims could contribute towards building the mosque.

Yes! Correct!

Next quiz question!

Can you guess which building here was the former Sultan's palace?

Istana Kampong Gelam was constructed in 1840 by the first Sultan's son. Today, it is preserved as the Malay Heritage Centre.

That one?

Right! It's now the Malay Heritage Centre.

Bingo again! Quiz me 10 more times! Please!

Err...Why don't we check out some street art first?

"Ooh...check out those funky murals!" Merry said as she dragged Marky towards the street art.

"Wefies!" Merry exclaimed, snapping several photos before anyone was ready.

"I've signed you up to try out traditional drums and pottery-making," Jewel said.

Merry drummed up a dreadful din with the djembe and her screechy singing.

She spun the pottery wheel at full speed, splashing clay on everyone around her. "Moulding bowls is making me want food!"

"Yes, it's a good time to fill our tummies!" Jewel said, determined not to let Merry ruffle her feathers.

Tahu telur

Nasi padang

Siput sedut

I'm full! Where are we going now?

I know who can keep up with Merry's energy levels!

"I thought you would enjoy meeting Marina," Merli said when they arrived at Sentosa.

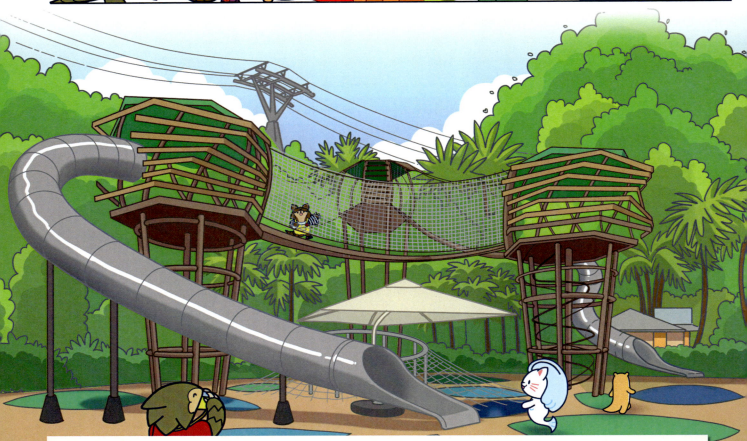

Nestopia is a unique open-air play space for an adrenaline-filled, family experience. Kids can climb and crawl to their heart's content at its 17 play sections fitted with challenging obstacle courses made up of three giant nests situated at 7.5 metres off the ground, with amazing views of the South China Sea, and two long slides.

At Nestopia, Marina was as energetic as Merry. They scaled the nets forwards, backwards and sideways. They climbed high to the giant nests. They went down the longest slides till they saw double.

"Let's check out Skyline Luge," Merry said to Marina.

"I love thrill rides!" Marina said as they made their way over.

Skyline Luge is a family-friendly gravity-fuelled thrill ride that brings you through a rainforest in unique 3-wheel Luge carts that travel down exciting tracks, with speed-controls that the driver is in full control of.

They hopped onto the skyride to get to the Luge station. The view was breathtaking!

They manoeuvred hairpin corners.

They careened through exhilarating tunnels.

And they whooped with delight as they raced downslope.

Meanwhile, Marky and Merli returned to Nestopia.

When Marky and Merli reached Skyline Luge, Merry and Marina had left already.

How are we going to find them?

We need a search party!

An otter and pangolin? They headed that way.

Mayday! We've lost Merry and Marina. Come quickly! We need all your help.

Thanks for coming!

Let's split up to find Merry and Marina.

D65, we need your high-level view!

Whee!!!

The family-friendly Mega Adventure is home to MegaZip, known as the most extreme zip line experience in Southeast Asia. It offers the thrill of soaring down its 450 metre long zip line at 60 km/hour (as fast as the horizontal speed of an eagle).

Meanwhile, Merry and Marina were playing at Palawan Beach.

"Check out this giant bouncy castle obstacle course!" Merry exclaimed.

"Let's see who's faster!" Marina cried as they raced.

HydroDash is Singapore's first floating aqua park. This huge family-friendly inflatable waterpark at Palawan Beach boasts epic obstacle courses with trampolines, springboards and slides, promising fun for all ages.

"Oops... I forgot," Merry said, turning red when she saw everyone staring at her. "Sorry, everyone."

"Sorry," Marina said sheepishly.

"I'm glad that we found you both," Merli said.

Singapore's hawker culture was inscribed on UNESCO's intangible culture heritage list in 2020. This living heritage is shared by both hawkers and patrons, and reflects Singapore's multicultural identity, with people from all walks of life dining and bonding over hawker food of different cultures.

COFFEE

Chinatown Complex and Food Centre has, through the years, served as the home of some of the street hawkers who used to ply their trade in the area, and still houses many traditional foods throughout its over 200 cooked food stalls.

"I ordered Nonya *bak chang*, satay *beehoon*, Hainanese chicken rice, claypot rice, *kueh pie tee*, *popiah*, *yong tau foo* and *chendol*," Chomp Chomp said. "Is that enough?"

"I'm stuffed like a turkey," Jewel said. "How about a walk around Chinatown?"

29

They passed two temples and a mosque. "Don't you think Singapore is such a multicultural feast?" Jewel said.

As they paused in front of a mural of a durian stall, Chomp Chomp said, "Shall we feast on the King of fruits?"

Painted by local artist Yip Yew Chong, this wall mural depicts Japanese anime character Detective Conan enjoying durian at a traditional street hawker stall. This special commission commemorated the movie release of *Detective Conan: The Fist of Blue Sapphire*, where the detective travels to Singapore.

"Thank you all for your patience with me," Merry said in between mouthfuls of durian.

Kind, thoughtful friends like you make things merry.

Went to some more cool places in Singapore with Merli and Merry!

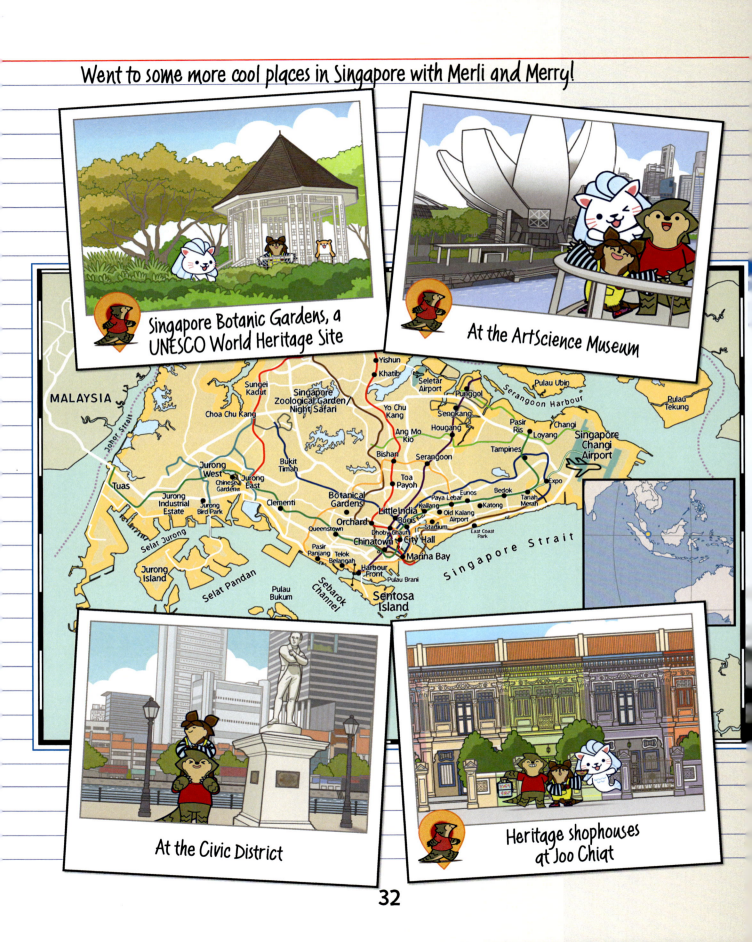

Singapore Botanic Gardens, a UNESCO World Heritage Site

At the ArtScience Museum

At the Civic District

Heritage shophouses at Joo Chiat

Getting henna done at
Little India Arcade

At Henderson Waves bridge

Shopping along Orchard Road

At National Gallery Singapore

Birdwatching at Sungei
Buloh Wetland Reserve

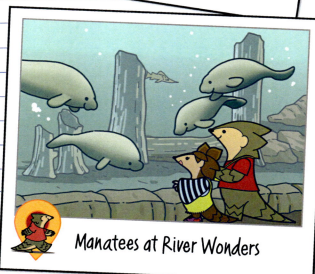
Manatees at River Wonders

Fun facts on animals that are residents in Singapore:

See if you can spot these local animals in the story!

Oriental pied hornbill

The oriental pied hornbill is now abundant in Singapore's urban areas and is often sighted in parks. Hornbills mate for life and exhibit fascinating breeding behaviour. When building a nest, the female enlarges a tree hole and cleans it. The nest entrance is plastered over with mud and other assorted materials such as fibres, leaving only a narrow slit. The female lays her eggs in the cavity and remains there with her hatchlings for about three months. During that time, they are entirely dependent on the male who can bring food to them up to 20 times a day.

Oriental pied hornbill

Smooth-coated Otter

Smooth-coated otters are commonly seen in some of the parks and waterways in Singapore. Otters live in closely-knit family groups. They use scent to mark their homes and "talk" to one another by making different calls to keep in touch! Otters have very sensitive paws and long whiskers to help them sense their surroundings and to hunt for fish, crayfish, crabs, mussels, frogs and even small birds.

Smooth-coated otter

Long-tailed macaque

The long-tailed macaque is the most common non-human primate species in Singapore.

They live in the nature reserves and forests, but may venture to the fringes and beyond to forage for food. Macaques are 'forest farmers'. They consume fruits and help to disperse seeds which germinate into new plants. When macaques switch to human food, they stop playing their role in maintaining the natural balance in the forests.

Long-tailed macaque

Reticulated python

Reticulated pythons are the world's longest snakes, with the longest ever recorded at 10 metres in length.

Commonly found in Southeast Asia, including countries like Singapore, pythons are non-venomous and kill by constricting prey to cut off their blood supply. They feed mainly on rats, frogs and birds, and play an important role in keeping rat populations in check.

Reticulated python

Estuarine crocodile

Estuarine crocodiles are found in the wild in Singapore, although they are not commonly sighted. Also known as the saltwater crocodile, it is one of the largest crocodile species in the world and can grow to more than 5 metres in length. The species is endangered due to the destruction of its habitats and over-hunting for its hide (valued as quality leather for making shoes and handbags) and meat.

Estuarine crocodile

Now, let's learn more about the Sunda pangolin:

Sunda pangolin

Sunda pangolins can be found in the forested areas of Singapore, where they feed on ants and termites. They use their long sticky tongue to slurp up insects. They are covered with an armour of scales, hence their other name 'scaly anteater'. When threatened, pangolins roll themselves into a ball to protect their non-scaly parts. Sunda pangolins are critically endangered as they are hunted illegally for their scales and flesh.

For Caleb, who inspires me with fun, comic ideas for Marky Polo's Travels
—E.L.L.

For Phoebe, Jaden, and Karen, let's explore more.
For Poh Zi Qun and teams, the designers of Merli and Friends. Thank you!
—N.L.

Published by
WS Education, an imprint of
World Scientific Publishing Co. Pte. Ltd.
5 Toh Tuck Link, Singapore 596224
USA office: 27 Warren Street, Suite 401-402, Hackensack, NJ 07601
UK office: 57 Shelton Street, Covent Garden, London WC2H 9HE

National Library Board, Singapore Cataloguing in Publication Data
Name(s): Lim, Emily, 1971– | Liem, Nicholas, illustrator.
Title: Marky Polo in Singapore / written by Emily Lim-Leh ; illustrated by Nicholas Liem.
Other Title(s): Marky Polo's travels ; Volume 3.
Description: Singapore : WS Education, [2023]
Identifier(s): ISBN 978-981-12-5880-0 (hardcover) | 978-981-12-5881-7 (paperback) |
978-981-12-5882-4 (ebook for institutions) | 978-981-12-5883-1 (ebook for individuals)
Subject(s): LCSH: Pangolins--Juvenile fiction. | Singapore--Juvenile fiction.
Classification: DDC 428.6--dc23

British Library Cataloguing-in-Publication Data
A catalogue record for this book is available from the British Library.

Desk Editor: Daniele Lee

Printed in Singapore

We wish to acknowledge the following organisations and individuals for their contributions to this book (names are listed in no particular order):
National Heritage Board, Urban Redevelopment Authority, Skyline Luge Sentosa, Sultan Mosque Management Board, Chinatown Business Association, Chinatown Complex Hawkers Merchant Association, Marina Bay Sands, Singapore Airlines (Batik motif scarf on back cover), Gardens by the Bay, Mega Adventure, Yip Yew Chong, iFly Singapore, National Gallery Singapore, Blu Jaz Café & Idris Johor, Jamae Chulia Mosque Management Board, Sri Mariamman Temple, Jewel Changi Airport Devt., Majlis Ugama Islam Singapura (MUIS), Mandai Wildlife Group, JTC Corporation, Didier Jaba Mathieu, National Parks Board, Shangri-La Group Hotels Singapore, HeadRock VR Singapore, Buddha Tooth Relic Temple & Museum, Little India Arcade and the Singapore Tourism Board.

Look out for more dynamic, full-colour illustrated children's books in this exciting series *Marky Polo's Travels.*

To receive updates about children's titles from WS Education, go to https://www.worldscientific.com/page/newsletter/subscribe, choose "Education", click on "Children's Books" and key in your email address.

Follow us @worldscientificedu on Instagram and @ World Scientific Education on YouTube for our latest releases, videos and promotions.

Visit Singapore at visitsingapore.com